For Mary Rife

Thank you to Grandma Kathy, who told us
this true story and showed us the real photograph.

Looking back, she felt that her mother dealt with her
fairly and that no one had a brother who loved her more.   —J.D.

Text © 1992 Joan Donaldson.   Illustrations © 1992 Tasha Tudor.   All rights reserved.
Published by Checkerboard Press, Inc., 30 Vesey Street, New York, NY 10007.
ISBN: 1-56288-158-2   Library of Congress Catalog Card Number: 91-73086   Printed in Singapore   0 9 8 7 6 5 4 3 2 1

The Real Pretend

By Joan Donaldson
Illustrated by Tasha Tudor

Checkerboard Press
New York

Kathy and her mother had been busy all morning picking and snapping green beans to put up for the winter. Now it was afternoon and her mother had shooed Kathy outside, away from the hot cookstove, while she canned the beans. Kathy sat kicking her heels against the chestnut tree stump in her front yard and watched a fussy wren scold her gray cat.

The day was hot and there was not much to do. Suddenly Kathy remembered the new Larkins catalog that had arrived in the mail. She liked looking at all the drawings of herbs and spices that Larkins sold. As Kathy paged through the catalog she had an idea: "I can pretend I'm selling groceries and visit our neighbors with the catalog. I'll get orders and pretend I'll deliver them later." Kathy ran into the house to get her blue notebook and red pencil. She tiptoed past the kitchen and out the front door—she certainly didn't want her mother to stop her.

Kathy skipped off to Mrs. Carroll's house first. Mrs. Carroll was busy cutting corn kernels from their cobs. She was happy to see Kathy. "Ah, little Kathy, what are you up to today?" she asked in her strong Irish brogue.

"Good afternoon, Mrs. Carroll," said Kathy in her most grown-up voice. "I thought you might be needing something from the Larkins catalog, so I've come by to take your order."

Mrs. Carroll smiled at Kathy. "So I do, dear," Mrs. Carroll said. "I could use a bit of baking powder, and does Larkins carry currants?" she asked as she thumbed through the catalog.

Kathy nodded and handed her notebook to Mrs. Carroll. "If you write your order here, you'll get exactly what you want."

"A fine Larkins employee you are, making the customers do the work!" Mrs. Carroll teased, and Kathy blushed.

Next Kathy visited Mrs. Rose, who
was taking down her laundry. She cheerfully joined in
Kathy's pretend. "I could use some nutmeg," she said thoughtfully.

"Will that be one pound or two?" Kathy asked.

"Heavens, child, my family likes rice pudding, but a pound of nutmeg would last ten
years!" she exclaimed. "A quarter pound will do nicely," she said, and wrote an order for
nutmeg, vanilla, cinnamon, and cloves in the notebook.

After Mrs. Rose, Kathy made her way to Mrs. Hubbard's and Mrs. MacDonald's houses, and
then she visited Miss Hill, who was to be her teacher when she started school the following week.
Her last call was at Mr. Williams's house. He liked to make ice cream, so Kathy thought he
might need some vanilla. Mr. Williams welcomed Kathy in and offered her some lemonade.
"So you are selling Larkins products these days, Kathy? Have you grown tired of being
a little girl?" he asked.

"Oh, no!" she said. "This is just pretend." Mr. Williams chuckled as he
wrote an order for vanilla, salt, and other goods.

"That's enough," thought Kathy as she left the house. She was hot and feeling tired, so she slowly trudged home.

Back home Kathy dropped her notebook and the Larkins catalog on a chair on the porch and went inside to see if supper was ready. Soon after, her older brother, Robert, returned from fishing and noticed Kathy's notebook and the catalog. "What's this?" he wondered.

As Robert slowly turned the pages of the little notebook, he realized what Kathy had been up to. Smiling, Robert took the notebook to his room. As a sixth grader, he was very proud of his penmanship, and he carefully wrote out an order. He sealed it in an envelope addressed to Larkins. "I'll send it to Larkins. It won't matter, as I'm not sending any money. They'll be very impressed that such a little girl could get so many orders. Maybe they'll write her a letter. She'd like that," he thought kindly.

The next day was Sunday, full of clean clothes and church. Kathy and her friends found it hard to be quiet. They whispered all through the service. School was starting the next day!

Then it was Monday—Kathy's very first day of school. She was very excited. And soon she and Robert were so busy at school—there was a lot to do and remember—that she forgot all about her Larkins game of pretend.

So it was quite a shock when Kathy and Robert's mother showed them a letter from Larkins a month later.

"Do either of you know anything about a Larkins order? This letter says that there's five dollars' worth of Larkins products at the post office that must be paid for," she said sternly. "What does this mean? What have you done?"

Kathy began to cry. Robert explained, "I found Kathy's notebook with the Larkins catalog and saw that she had made up a pretend about selling Larkins products. I thought it would be fun to send off the orders that Kathy had taken from the neighbors. But I never thought this would happen," he said in a worried voice.

"Oh, Robert!" His mother shook her head. "There's no way I can find the money. Why didn't you ask my permission before you played this silly game? You two put yourselves into this scrape, and now you must work together to find your way out of it."

The children took the Larkins letter from their mother and reluctantly left the house to go and talk to each neighbor. They headed for Mrs. Hubbard's. "You know, Kathy, Mrs. Hubbard has four sons and she must cook a lot. Maybe she will need the spices." Cinnamon smells filled the air as they knocked on her door. When she opened the door, the children explained what had happened.

"I could have used the cinnamon earlier today for the rolls I am baking now. But I'll still need some, so I'll certainly buy the cinnamon," Mrs. Hubbard said. "Well, I guess this prank is no worse than some my own boys got up to when they were your age, Kathy," she added as she gave Kathy and Robert the money and sent them on their way.

Then they went to Mrs. Carroll's. Luckily Mrs. Rose was visiting her. The women listened as Robert related the problem. Mrs. Carroll broke out laughing. "Robert, my lad, what a way to start a business career! I'll gladly buy the groceries, but next time, Kathy, let's be sure to keep it real pretend."

Mrs. Rose agreed with a smile. "You two must keep your mother on her toes. Good luck in explaining this to the other neighbors," she said as she paid them.

"We mustn't forget Mrs. MacDonald," Kathy said as she glanced at the Larkins order form. "She asked for ginger, cloves, and allspice."

"I bet she uses those spices in the molasses cookies Larry brings fishing," remarked Robert. "Let's go visit her next."

Mrs. MacDonald was busy picking pears and could only stop and listen for a moment. "Such an imagination you have, Kathy!" she exclaimed. "Run to the house and tell Larry I said to give you the money."

Relieved, the children left Mrs. MacDonald's and made their way to the home of Miss Hill, Kathy's teacher. Her eyes sparkled with amusement as Kathy explained what had happened.

"I never thought the order was real," she said. "It's a good thing the package arrived after my first paycheck. I'm not sure I would have chosen spices over the red calico I planned to buy this afternoon to make a new dress," she added as she counted out the coins to pay for her order.

Their last stop was Mr. Williams's house. He laughed
loudly at their tale of woe. "Someday—when you've learned all
your letters—you should write this down so that other children will learn
from your adventure," he told Kathy. "Now get along with you, and don't forget
you're invited to help me make ice cream when I get my vanilla!"

Tired but relieved, Kathy and Robert walked to the post office to pay for the Larkins order.
After paying five dollars they were surprised to find they still had some money left over. When
they arrived home, Kathy ran to her mother.

"We paid for the whole order, but we still have money left over! Somebody must have paid too
much," she said.

"The extra money is yours to keep," explained their mother. "When you sell products for
Larkins, they let you keep a little of the money you collect as a wage for the work
you did. It's called a commission. After you have delivered the orders, you
may spend the extra money as you please on the weekend."

The next Saturday, as Robert and Kathy walked to town, she
asked him, "What do you plan to buy, Robert?"

"I could use a new bobber or two. And I'd like a few of those brass fish hooks. How
about you, Kathy?"

"I'd love a new hat or muff. But if there isn't enough money, I guess one of those tiny china
dolls and lots of candy!"

Holding hands, the pair crossed the street and entered Dickinson's Mercantile. Robert headed
toward the fishing gear, while Kathy made for the hat counter.

"Robert, look at me," called Kathy as she tried on one hat after another. Robert grinned
and put down the tackle. He walked over to Kathy and asked, "Of all these hats, if you
could choose just one, which would it be?"

"Oh, the beaver one," said Kathy.

Suddenly Robert realized it would take all the money they had to satisfy Kathy.
With a burst of brotherly love, and feeling very grand, Robert motioned to the clerk.
"We'll take this one, ma'am," he said.

Beaming, Kathy flung her arms around her brother.

Just as they left the store, Robert spied the pony man who took photographs of people on his pony. "Please, sir, all I have is a nickel, but could you take my sister's picture with her new hat?"

The pony man smiled. As Robert admired his little sister, the pony man swung Kathy onto the pony and in a puff of smoke captured the glory of her new hat, her love for her brother, and the sweetness of her small world.